FLY LITTLE BIRD, FLY!

The True Story of Oliver Nordmark &
America's Orphan Trains

Donna Nordmark Aviles

For Kyla,
Enjoy!
Donna N. Aviles

Wasteland Press
Shelbyville, KY USA
www.wastelandpress.net

Fly Little Bird, Fly! The True Story Of Oliver Nordmark & America's Orphan Trains
By Donna Nordmark Aviles
www.orphantrainbook.com

Third Printing – April 2010
ISBN: 1-932852-07-7

Printed in the U.S.A.

For my father, Benjamin Nordmark, who took the time to listen to and share the stories of Oliver's childhood. I thank him for leading by example.

And to my daughter, Estella Aviles and my sister, Allison Bricker, both of whom were instrumental in seeing this book to its completion.

Oliver Nordmark, Circa 1913, Age 15 (Esbon, Kansas)

INTRODUCTION

In 1853 Reverend Charles Loring Brace established the Children's Aid Society in an effort to help the estimated 30,000 homeless and neglected children living in New York City. Between 1854 and 1929, over 100,000 children were sent by the Society to farming communities in the Midwest in search of homes. It was believed that the farmers would welcome the children and take them into their families. In return, the children would supply much needed help with the labors of farm life. Later known as The Orphan Train Movement, this was, in fact, the forerunner of today's foster care system.

This book is the true story of my grandfather, Oliver Nordmark, and his younger brother Edward. Together they rode one of America's orphan trains from New York City to Kansas in 1906. Oliver was just eight years old and believed that he and Edward had been orphaned. Documents found when he was a grown man, however, proved otherwise. Their mother Lizzie died in 1911 when Oliver was thirteen and their father Otto died when he was nine years old.

Oliver married Estella Rarick and together they had six children, eventually settling down in Stroudsburg, Pennsylvania. After Estella's sudden death, Oliver was left to care for his children in the midst of The Great Depression. Try as he might, he was unsuccessful at keeping his young family together and his own children were placed in foster care through The Children's Aid Society.

Oliver died at the age of ninety-five after being hit by a car while riding his bicycle. Although he did drive, and in fact traveled all around the United States in his retirement, I always remember him having and riding his bike. I suppose from the first time he saw one as a young boy he remained fascinated by them. Oliver is survived by four of his six children, twenty-three grandchildren and numerous great-grandchildren.

I am honored to have known him and I thank him for sharing his story. I hope you enjoy it!

-Donna Nordmark Aviles

CHAPTER ONE
HEADING WEST, THINKING BACK

Oliver sat in the doorway of the moving boxcar soaking up the warmth of the August sun. As the car chugged along, he swung his legs to the rhythm of the squeaking rails. Any passerby along the tracks might presume that the small boy had not a care in the world. Oliver looked at the situation he presently found himself in as the start of a big adventure – maybe the biggest adventure of his life! Watching the scenery unfold before him, he saw sights he never even knew existed. Having never left New York City in all his seven years, he was amazed at the openness and gently rolling hills of the grasslands before him. They seemed to Oliver to extend as far as the eye could see. He wondered if the place where the blue sky met the tall grass was the beginning of Heaven. If he walked to that place, would he again see his mother's worn and tired face? It seemed so beautiful there.... would his mother be smiling at last, free of whatever had caused her such sorrow in New York City?

Every now and then the train slowed to a near crawl as it passed through small villages etched out of the dust and grass. Each village had a weather beaten wooden platform next to the tracks, but only once so far had Oliver seen people waiting on the platform. His train never stopped at the platforms, so he began to know that somehow, this was a special train carrying special children. He counted himself and his brother Edward, three years his junior, among these special people. Oliver glanced at Edward as he slept soundly on a thin layer of straw just inside the boxcar door. Instinctively, he knew that he was now his brother's keeper.

As he sat and soaked it all in, breathing deeply of the fresh, fragrant air, he couldn't help but think of his eighth birthday just two months away. Although he hadn't a clue as to where he was headed, he did know where he had been. He had turned seven just ten short months ago on October 8, 1905. His teacher, Mrs. Petty (or Mrs. Pretty as Oliver secretly called her) had brought a small chocolate cake to school and placed it right in front of him on his desk. She led the class in "Happy Birthday To You" and asked him if he would like to share his cake with the other students. "NO, NO, a hundred times NO," thought Oliver to himself.

Aloud, however, he said, "If you think I should Mrs. Pret….ah...Petty."

Oliver's heart sank in his chest as he watched Mrs. Petty take his cake to her desk and carefully slice it into small pieces; one for each of his classmates. As his hand brought the first bite to his lips, Oliver thought it must be the most delicious confection he had ever tasted. He savored every crumb, all the time thinking that Mrs. Petty must really think he was something special to bake him a cake. His own mother had never done that.

Thinking back to that happy day, Oliver's thoughts drifted back to his home – the only real home he had ever had. *405 East 19th Street, New York, New York.* His mother, Elizabeth - or Lizzie as everyone called her - had made him memorize his address for as long as he could remember.

"Just in case you get lost, Oliver. You can tell any shopkeeper and they will help you find your way," she used to say.

Of course Oliver knew he would never get lost. He knew his neighborhood like the back of his hand. He even knew how to get to Madison Avenue and back. Oliver's father, Otto, was a tailor by trade. He worked in the main room of the family's three room apartment. His big tailor's table took up most of the room. Handmade racks that his father had built stood along the sides of the room. These racks held the finished work of his father's trade and were used to transport those suits to the fancy shops of

Madison Avenue. Otto had trusted his oldest son, at the tender age of six, to push those racks all the way to Madison. Oliver felt proud and very grown up to be delivering his father's suits – very fine suits indeed, he was sure of that.

Oliver tried to think back as far as he could remember.....when had things begun to change? Not long after that happy day at school on his seventh birthday, Oliver had overheard some of the bigger boys in the schoolyard talking about playing "hooky" from school. Having never even heard of "hooky", he had listened intently as they joked about all the fun they had and how they were going to do it again. From what he could gather, it seemed to Oliver that hooky was something every kid should try. It was like a holiday from school, except the kid got to decide when the holiday would be. He wondered why Mrs. Petty hadn't mentioned this to the class. Maybe she had explained it when he was home sick with that terrible fever at the start of school. Yes, that must be it. She just forgot that Oliver had not been there when she explained it. Well, he certainly did not want to point out to his pretty young teacher that she had made a mistake. So on his own, Oliver decided when his "hooky day" would be. Tomorrow, of course! Tomorrow would be a perfect day for hooky!

The next morning was a sunny and cool Thursday near the end of October. Oliver woke early filled with excitement about his hooky day, as he was now calling it to himself. He quickly dressed in his knickers and sweater, pulled on his cap and grabbed a few spoonfuls of oatmeal that his mother had set out for him.

As he ran down the steps of the apartment building, his mother called out from the open door, "Oliver, your books!"

"I don't need them today!" he shouted back over his shoulder. He could hear continued protests from his mother but he didn't stop to explain. This was one day he didn't want to be late!

Arriving at the school yard, Oliver waited for the ringing of the loud bell which signaled the start of the school day. He watched as his schoolmates filed into the building, their book straps over their shoulders and tin lunch buckets in their hands.

With a bounce in his step and a whistle on his lips, the happy first grader frolicked up and down the block in front of his school. His own hooky day! What fun, indeed! Oliver skipped a stone, kicked a dirty old bottle, and was thoroughly enjoying his day of freedom in the crisp autumn air. Not long after he had begun his holiday, he heard a shout from a second story school window.

"Hey, what are you doing?" a boy called out to Oliver.

Grinning from ear to ear, Oliver replied, "Having my hooky day, it's great!"

Later that day, as the school children filed out to the yard to eat from their lunch pails, Oliver heard his name.

"Oliver Nordmark!" called out Mrs. Petty. "What in the world are you up to?"

Looking only slightly confused, Oliver responded, "I'm having my hooky day!" Her faced turned red in anger. Now he was *really* confused.

"Get in here right this instant!" she screamed at him.

Not knowing what to do, and not liking the look on his teacher's face, Oliver decided he'd better listen. He walked onto the schoolyard with his head down. Mrs. Petty grabbed him by the ear and pulled him into the building.

Marching him into the first grade classroom, she shouted to Oliver, "Hold out your hands!"

With a quivering lip, Oliver slowly raised his arms, hands extended. Before he could make any sense of what was happening, Mrs. Petty reached for her yardstick and cracked him on the knuckles just as hard as she could. *Crack! Crack! Crack!* Wincing in pain, Oliver tried hard to hold back every tear.

CHAPTER TWO

OLIVER GOES TO PRISON

"You know," Oliver now thought to himself as he looked out over the passing prairie, "I think that was the ruination of me, right then and there. Hooky day, my eye! Yes, I do believe that was the start of *all* this."

He was right, of course. The very next day at school, Oliver was called out of his class to the Headmaster's office. As he entered, he noticed a tall man in a rumpled suit with thin stripes. The man's shoes were scuffed and he carried a brown case that looked to Oliver like a small suitcase.

The man looked Oliver square in the eye and spoke firmly, "Delinquency will not be tolerated in our schools, young man. You will be coming with me for a period of detention in an effort to correct your behavior."

Oliver just gave the man a puzzled look but decided he had better do as he was told to avoid any more trouble. Silently, he followed the man out of the building.

****

Edward stirred in the hay next to Oliver, momentarily breaking his chain of thought.

"I'm hungry," Edward whispered as he looked up through glassy eyes.

"There's nothing to eat yet," replied Oliver. As he looked down at Edward's tiny face about to cry, Oliver reached into his pocket and took out half a gingersnap. "Here," he said, handing the treat to Edward. "This is the last I have."

Edward promptly sat up and joined his big brother at the edge of the boxcar. As he quietly enjoyed his treat, Oliver's arm reached around his brother's shoulder. Somewhere in his mind, Oliver knew that giving Edward his last gingersnap was only the beginning of the many sacrifices that lay ahead. After all, who else did Edward have now? He was only a boy of four. Who would look out for him if not Oliver?

****

Having calmed Edward with the gingersnap, Oliver's mind wandered back to the tall man in the suit. Oliver had ridden that day in the man's horse-drawn buggy, through the streets of New York City to a tall skyscraper building. Above the front door were the words "GUARISH SOCIETY". He wondered what that might mean. He was taken to a room on the 9th floor. He remembered that because he had counted, at the top of each staircase, all the doors that they *didn't* enter. At the 9th door, the man took a large key from his pocket, opened the door, and led Oliver to a room on the left side of the dimly lit hallway. It was a small room with one window. There were six small metal beds with old straw mattresses. There were no sheets and no pillows. Oliver looked around for blankets but found none. In fact, there was nothing else in the room. To Oliver, it looked like a prison. Although he had never seen a prison, he was sure that this is what one must look like. Without a word, the man left the room, closing and locking the door behind him. *Bang! Clang!*

"Yep," thought Oliver, "I'm in prison."

Oliver walked slowly around the dirty room looking into every nook and cranny. There were many kinds of bugs scurrying in the corners. That didn't bother him much. Oliver had seen so many bugs in his apartment building that he didn't think much about them....just a part of life. He climbed up on the furthest bed and looked out through the bars of the small window.

"Wow!" he heard himself say out loud to no one. "I can see all of New York City from here!"

What a great distraction. Oliver quickly forgot all about his troubles and reached his neck as far as he could to see as much as possible. Looking straight down, he saw something quite odd. There below him, in a vacant lot, was something moving around in circles. But what was it? It looked like little monkeys moving around on three wheels. There was one big wheel in front and two smaller wheels in the back. The monkeys were holding on to something, but Oliver couldn't quite make out just what. He stood on his tip toes watching the monkeys for what seemed like a long time, when suddenly the door to his prison opened up and three boys came in. The door slammed behind them.

Oliver was pretty sure that these boys were older than he was, but he managed a slight grin and said, "Hi, I'm Oliver."

"Well get down off my bed Oliver, and don't go near it again! I'm George and I'm in charge in *this* room. Now don't you forget it!"

"I'm sorry," Oliver replied. "I was just watching them monkeys down in that lot goin' round and round."

George looked sideways at Oliver, then walked over and looked out the window. "Monkeys?" he looked at Oliver with distain. "What are you, stupid or somethin'? Those ain't no monkeys. That's boys on bicycles. Boys who are *not* in trouble, like you are. Now sit on your own bed and shut up."

Oliver did as he was told and sat down quietly on the bed furthest from George's. He thought about what George had said – boys riding bicycles. Oliver had never seen a bicycle in his life. Boys rode them. Hmmm. I'm going to have a bicycle some day, he thought to himself. The fun of watching the monkeys, as he had imagined they were, was over. Over for good. This was prison and there would be no fun with monkeys – imagined or real.

Oliver remembered staying in the prison for about a week. He was fed two meals each day. The first meal was a runny oatmeal that tasted very bland. His mother had always added a little sugar. But there was no sugar in prison. Later in the day, the boys were fed soup broth that sometimes had things floating in it. His mother had sometimes put chunks of ham and vegetables in the soup she made. There was no ham, or meat of any kind, in prison. Oliver hoped that it might be bits of vegetables that he dodged with his spoon, but just to be sure, he never ate anything he didn't recognize as edible. Sometimes there was a hard crust of bread that came with the broth. Oliver would dip this in his bowl to make it a little softer before eating it. At home, he would spread a small pat of vegetable oil, hardened like butter, onto his bread. Bread, if served at all, was served stale and plain in prison. But Oliver ate it anyway. His hungry stomach wouldn't let him pass it up.

CHAPTER THREE
ORPHANAGE BOUND

As the week passed, there was no change in Oliver's daily prison routine. Most of his time was spent either sleeping, sitting on his bed daydreaming, or eating his meager meals. Twice during the week the guard came and led the boys down the metal stairs and outside to a small fenced lot where they were led in basic exercises. Oliver was happy to at least be out in the fresh air. He followed along with the exercises as best he could wondering just how long he was going to be in jail……until he was ten?.....until he was a grown-up?......until he died? His answer came that Saturday morning.

Just as he was getting ready to follow the other boys to the big room for his breakfast, the door to the cell slammed open. Oliver was truly giddy by the sight before him. He saw an older woman in a long grey dress. She wore a white apron over her dress and a grey and white cap in her hair. She stood behind a man in a striped suit. It was the same man who had called him out of Mrs. Petty's classroom and brought him to prison. But neither the man nor the woman was the reason for Oliver's glee. It was what the woman carried that spread a smile so wide across his face that Oliver thought he might just burst. Edward, his baby brother just three years old, was resting on the woman's hip. His blond curls lay across her shoulder and he wore nothing but his diaper and a pair of socks. A small wool blanket was draped around his tiny shoulders.

"Edward! My brother Edward!" Oliver shouted excitedly. He ran to hug Edward who instinctively reached out for him.

The woman never spoke, and she would not bend down for the boys to greet one another. A quick thought passed through Oliver's mind. They couldn't be putting Edward in jail too, could they? He was much too little to be here. No, no, something else must be going on here. So many thoughts were running through Oliver's mind that he couldn't settle on just one. Very abruptly, the tall man supplied the answer.

"Come with us now Oliver. I'm afraid your mother has died and your father is nowhere to be found. You and Edward are orphans now. Mrs. Thompson and I will be escorting both of you to The Children's Village Orphanage. That's where you'll be living from now on."

"What about my big sister Anna?" Oliver managed to quietly ask, trying to digest the meaning of the man's simply stated facts.

“Anna, being a girl, has been transferred to the Catholic Protectory for Girls in the Bronx section of New York City,” he offered flatly.

Well, thought Oliver, I guess that is that. We are orphans and we will live in an orphanage. It would at least be better than jail, he was sure of that. Maybe he would even get enough food, and maybe it would even be good food. He dared to dream. So many thoughts rushed around in his head….his mother had died…. how had that happened? ....was that why no one had come for him in prison? ....at least he had Edward….his father was nowhere to be found? ....would his father be able to find them in the orphanage? ....was his father dead too? ....this was all nearly too much for his young mind.

Oliver peered out the window of the man’s carriage as he traveled with Edward through the streets of New York City. He wasn’t near his neighborhood so Oliver really had no idea how far they had gone or in what direction they were headed. Edward nodded off as he rested his head against Oliver’s arm. After nearly a week in prison, it felt good to have his little brother so close. As the carriage pulled into a long drive, Oliver’s stomach began to growl and he realized that he had not eaten yet.

“We’re here,” stated Mrs. Thompson.

Oliver wriggled in his seat trying to make himself taller to see what was before them. His wriggling stirred Edward who rubbed his eyes and hung onto Oliver's arm.

"Mum…where's Mum?" Edward mumbled sleepily. Looking down at his blond curls, Oliver decided not to answer. He couldn't make sense of any of this himself. How could he be expected to explain it to Edward?

The carriage door opened and as Oliver stepped out, Mrs. Thompson scooped Edward up and headed toward the door of the orphanage. Oliver fell in behind as they entered the main hall. Once inside, they were greeted by an older woman. She took Edward from Mrs. Thompson.

"Well, you just come with me little fellow. I'll get you some nice warm clothes and a hot lunch. How does that sound?" she cooed to Edward.

"What about me?" Oliver spoke just above a whisper. "I'm hungry too."

"You'll be going with Matron O'Brien to the school age cottages," replied the older woman. "She'll be along for you shortly."

With that she disappeared down the long hall with Edward in her arms. Oliver had no idea that it would be nearly a year before he would see the sweet face and blond curls of his baby brother again.

Sitting down on a long wooden bench in the hallway, Oliver began idly counting the graying tiles of the floor.

"Come along now Oliver," called Mrs. Thompson. Her sudden, sharp voice startled Oliver from his daydreaming. She had been in a nearby office, along with the tall man in the striped suit. A large woman in a uniform was with her. Oliver figured that this must be Matron O'Brien. The four of them exited through the big front door and down the stone steps. Mrs. Thompson and the tall man reached for the carriage door handles, but only Mrs. Thompson glanced back to look at him.

"Good-bye Oliver. Good luck." She climbed into the carriage and off they went.

Oliver turned to look at Matron O'Brien. He was momentarily startled to see that she had already started walking down the path alongside the big building. He quickly ran to catch up with her. Walking along the path, Oliver was distracted by all he saw around him. There were small houses, like cottages, situated along the path. Some sat right near the path while others were further back on paths of their own. There were tall trees with leaves of burnt orange, red and yellow. Fallen leaves lay scattered on the ground everywhere he looked. Oliver took a deep breath that filled his head with all the smells of autumn. Matron O'Brien took a sharp turn onto a side path and quickly reached the door of cottage number 214. The number was carved in the wood of the front door.

Finally she spoke. "Now, this is your new home Oliver - number 214 of the school boys' cottages."

They crossed the threshold and entered the front room. Oliver quickly scanned the room, noticing a long table with lots of straight chairs along the back wall. He also saw a large fireplace with logs neatly stacked to one side. There were smaller tables and chairs in the front part of the room with books in the center of each table. There were colorful curtains hanging from the windows, and woven rugs covering large areas of the wooden floor boards. Along the left side of the room, just inside the front door, Oliver saw a row of large hooks. Dark blue coats hung from nearly every hook and there were boots on the floor under each coat. Everything seemed very clean to Oliver, having just spent the better part of a week in a bug infested jail cell.

"Now this is our cottage main room," began Matron O'Brien. "This is where you and your housemates do your lessons. We have meals there on the back table – breakfast, lunch and dinner. If you are late for meals, you do not eat. Is that understood?"

"Yes, Matron O'Brien. I won't be late," Oliver quickly replied.

"Your sleeping quarters are upstairs. Follow me," continued Matron O'Brien.

Oliver climbed the curved staircase staying close on Matron O'Brien's heals. Reaching the top stair, Oliver looked around, very pleased by what he saw. Unlike the jail he had just left, there were no straw mattresses devoid of bedding and pillows. No, this was just the opposite. On each wall he saw five beds. Each bed was painted white and had a real mattress. The mattresses were covered with blue blankets and pillows in white cases. Next to each bed was a white metal cabinet, tall and narrow. There were windows on each side of the room with blue and white checked curtains pulled back to let in the light of the day. A large oval shaped, braided rug covered the wooden floor boards in the center of the room. Matron O'Brien led Oliver to the far bed on the right side of the room.

"This will be your bed and clothes locker. You are responsible for keeping this bed perfectly made, without a wrinkle, just the way you see it now." Swinging the door of the cabinet open, she continued, "These are your uniforms. There are two shirts, two knickers, and one set of bed clothes. You are to wear each shirt and knickers for three days. On the fourth day you are to place your dirty uniform in the laundry cart over there." She pointed to the left of the staircase where, indeed, there stood a white cart. "By the time you wear your second uniform for three days, your first uniform will be back clean from the laundry." Matron O'Brien headed for the stairs. Calling over her shoulder, she further instructed Oliver, "Now change into your uniform and meet me downstairs. Your housemates will be returning from their morning chores shortly and we will be preparing our noon meal." With that, she disappeared down the stairs.

Oliver looked around. He opened his cabinet and looked inside. Everything was there, even a pair of brown shoes. He gently slid his fingertips across the neatly made, wrinkle free bed. Picking up the small pillow, he brought it to his chest and buried his little boy's face into the cushion of feathers. Tears slowly spilled from Oliver's eyes into the soft white case. The gravity of his situation began to sink in. He was in a strange place, with strange people, strange rules, and no idea what to do next. His thoughts turned to Edward. Did Edward have a bed to make each morning, free of wrinkles? Oliver was fairly certain that Edward would not even know what a wrinkle was, let alone how to make them go away.

"Oh Mum," Oliver's quivering lips whispered through his tears, "I'm scared, Mum."

CHAPTER FOUR
LIFE AT THE ORPHANAGE

Oliver's short-lived joy at seeing his young brother Edward was quickly replaced with a sad longing for all he had lost. Life in the orphanage cottage under the supervision of Matron O'Brien was very strict and constantly supervised. Each morning the boys would rise at 6:00 AM to the sound of a loud bell. They went to the washroom where bowls of room temperature water sat lined up on a wobbly table. Each boy quickly washed up with a coarse, scent free soap. They scrubbed their teeth with baking soda, then scurried back to their room to replace their nightshirts with uniforms. At the tone of the second bell, all ten boys lined up at attention across the front of their room. Matron O'Brien would pass along the line with a long pointer in her hand. She looked every boy up and down, inspecting uniforms, checking for clean hands and faces, and making sure everyone's hair had been combed into place. After the inspection, the boys filed down the stairs to the breakfast table.

Meal times passed in silence, no talking was allowed. Whatever food arrived on the plate in front of the boys, they were required to eat it, no questions asked. And eat it they did! The boys were kept so busy, and worked so hard at chores that they were always hungry. Second helpings of food did not exist. When the meal was finished, it was finished. Oliver really didn't mind the taste of most of the meals served in cottage number 214. His mother had never been an elaborate cook, mostly because there was not a lot of money to cook anything fancy. Her meals were tasty and filling, just not fancy. If something was served at the orphanage that he truly did not like, Oliver would close his eyes and imagine his mother's oatmeal with sugar, or her stew with turnips, and pretend that the meal in front of him tasted as good.

Months passed at cottage number 214 and before Oliver knew it, winter had arrived. Snow covered the grounds of the orphanage and the boys were kept busy with shoveling snow, cutting wood, and gathering enough kindling to keep their cottage warm. Fires were kept burning in the main room's fireplace during the day. At night, however, the fire went out and the boys were often chilled to the bone as they tried to sleep in the second floor bedroom.

As Oliver rode along on the train headed west, the long low calling of the steam engine's whistle rang though his head. It quickly reminded him of another whistle that sounded that cold winter at the orphanage. The first time he had heard it, he quickly turned to his housemate William, who was helping him shovel the front walk.

"What does that whistle mean?" Oliver fearfully asked.

"That's the whistle from the powerhouse," William replied. "They have a jail inside the powerhouse and they sound the whistle every time someone gets sent to the jail for breaking a rule."

Oliver looked over at William, "Any rule?" he wondered aloud.

"*Any* rule," was William's reply of warning.

Oliver finished his shoveling knowing full well that he would not be breaking any rules. Having already been to jail, he was going to make sure, no matter what, he never ended up there again.

Oh, if only he had known! The very next morning, Oliver and his housemates woke to the 6:00 AM bell. As he rubbed his sleepy eyes to see the light of day, Oliver noticed that he not only saw light, but he could also see his breath! It had gotten so could during the night that Oliver's skin was covered with goose pimples and his ears were ice cold. Returning from the washroom, Oliver had what he thought was a brilliant idea. Since his clean uniform had come back just the evening before, and he still had one day left to wear his current uniform before it had to go in the laundry, Oliver decided to put both his shirts on to try to fend off the cold. Standing nice and tall in the inspection line, Oliver held back a grin of pride at having been so clever. As Matron O'Brien passed in front of him, she stopped abruptly.

"Oliver Nordmark! What do you think you are doing?" She pulled Oliver by the arm over to his bed. "Remove that shirt!" she barked at him. Oliver unbuttoned his shirt, revealing the second shirt underneath. "You have broken the uniform rules, young man. It's the jailhouse for you!"

She took Oliver by the arm and escorted him all the way to the powerhouse. As she pushed him through the door, she stated firmly, "Rules are made to be followed, Oliver. The sooner you accept that in life the better off you'll be."

The heavy door slammed behind him and the powerhouse whistle sounded for the arrival of another captive orphan.

CHAPTER FIVE

THE POWERHOUSE JAIL

Turning from the slammed door, Oliver looked into the jail. He was surprised by what he saw. There were several windows on each wall that were covered with thick, black iron bars in a criss-cross pattern. There was a big ring painted on the floor of the open room. Oliver did not see any cell doors around the room. Boys of all ages milled about inside the ring. Men in uniforms with big sticks stood around the outside of the ring. Before he could even open his mouth to speak, one of the guards took him roughly by the elbow and shoved him into the ring.

"Stay inside the ring unless you wanta get beat!" the guard shouted. Oliver walked quickly and quietly to the center of the ring, trying not to be noticed. He fought back a tear and tried to look brave.

"Don't pay no 'tention to him," a tall boy of about ten said to Oliver. "He ain't never beat no one yet, far as I can tell."

Breathing a short sigh of relief, Oliver looked around for a familiar face. Sadly, he found none. Within a few minutes, there were loud banging and clanging noises and all the boys dropped down to a sitting position. Oliver quickly did the same, not wishing to stand out. Big metal carts were being pushed to the edge of the circle where the guards grabbed the trays from inside and hurriedly passed them among the seated boys. Ah, breakfast, Oliver thought to himself. He quickly devoured the lukewarm mush. It was runny and tasteless but filled his small stomach nonetheless. A guard's stick banging against the metal cart signaled the end of breakfast and all the boys slid their trays to the edge of the circle. The guard swatted his stick on the shoulders of two boys sitting near the circle's edge. They leapt to their feet and began scurrying around the circle, picking up and stacking the trays back into the cart. When the task was complete, they quickly returned to the ring.

Around mid-morning, a shrill bell sounded and all the boys lay on their backs in straight lines. Again, Oliver moved as quickly as possible to find a line with room for him, so as not to stand out. Within seconds, a guard began pacing back and forth along one side of the ring shouting out different exercises for the boys to do.

"Sit ups!" he bellowed. "One, Two, Three, Four, One Two, Three, Four!"

Oliver tried to keep up with the other boys. He was sure he skipped one every now and then but hoped that the guard would not notice.

"On your stomachs!" was the guard's next command. "Push ups!" he shouted over their heads. "One, Two, Three, Four, One, Two, Three, Four!"

This went on for so long that Oliver thought he would collapse from exhaustion. He hung in there as best he could and counted his blessings that he was not singled out for cheating when he got behind on the count. Finally, the bell sounded again and all the boys stood up and began mingling about.

After a lunch which followed the same routine as breakfast, the guards began escorting the boys in groups of four to the bathroom. There were no doors to the bathroom, and Oliver was embarrassed to find that the guard stood watch over them the whole time. With his head down, he quickly went about his business and returned to the ring. He was certain that his face was red as a beet!

As the day wore on, and night approached, the guards pushed woven mats into the ring. The boys each grabbed a mat and spread them out on the floor of the ring. Curling up on his mat, Oliver briefly thought about asking for a blanket, but immediately dismissed the idea. If he had learned nothing else over the past several months, he had certainly learned that asking questions and breaking even the smallest of rules was a devastatingly bad idea.

Two days and two nights came and went for Oliver inside the ring of the powerhouse jail. On the morning of the third day, his name was called and he was escorted back to cottage number 214.

"Well, that sure learned me a lesson," he mumbled under his breath. He never thought he would be so happy to see his housemates and his own *real* mattress!

For the rest of that winter, Oliver managed to keep from getting into any further trouble. He followed every rule to the very letter. He wore one shirt, and one pair of knickers – no matter what. He made his bed each morning without so much as a single wrinkle. He completed his chores without skipping any steps and always finished on time. His meals were eaten in silence, never commenting on the taste and never asking for seconds.

As winter slowly turned to spring, Oliver looked forward each day to the half hour that the boys were allowed to be on the playground. He loved swinging on the swings, tipping his head back as far as he could with his eyes closed. It made him feel like he hadn't a care in the world. He could pretend that his life was very different as long as his eyes were closed. Sometimes he imagined he was back on East 19th Street helping his father push the suit racks. He imagined his sister Anna helping his mother in the kitchen and little Edward standing in his crib. Sometimes he pretended that he was someone else all together.... Someone who lived in a fancy house with a loving mother and father.... Someone who had one of those bicycles he had seen so long ago from the Guarish Society Prison. It was fun pretending.

It was just one such spring day that Oliver and his housemates watched as a tall, skinny kid that everyone called "Daddy Long Legs" took off like a shot from the playground. He was trying to run away, and in fact, he almost succeeded. Secretly, the boys on the playground cheered him on. Within just ten minutes though, the boys could see across the field to where the runaway was being escorted by two guards back to the orphanage, hands held behind his back.

As the boys stood silent, Oliver called out, "Hi Daddy Long Legs!"

The other boys sounded an audible gasp as one of the guards ran over and took Oliver by the scruff of the neck, dragging him away with the runaway.

"Now *that one* cost me a whole week in that powerhouse jail!" Oliver said out loud to no one but Edward, who was now resting back in the hay of the boxcar. "A whole week just for saying that!"

CHAPTER SIX

THE ORPHANS RIDE WEST

"All right children, sit up. Its time for some lunch," called the friendly voice of one of the matrons accompanying the orphans on their train ride.

Oliver pulled his feet in from the edge of the boxcar and scooted across the hay next to Edward who was already reaching for his portion. The matron handed each child a tin bowl and cup. Following behind her was a second woman who poured a ladle full of thin soup into each bowl. A crust of bread and warm milk in their cups completed the meal.

"Pretty good soup, huh Edward?" Oliver asked his brother, offering a cheerful smile.

Edward raised his eyes to Oliver as he sipped from his soup bowl, his head bobbing up and down in approval. Wondering again what lay ahead for them, Oliver thought about their last day at the orphanage....

****

“Give me your attention boys,” Matron O’Brien commanded as she stood over the table at last night’s dinner. “There has been a decision made by The Children’s Aid Society that affects many of the children living here at the orphanage. It seems that due to overcrowding, many of you are going to be resettled with families in the Western Territory. If your name is called, you are to meet your escort in front of the Administration Building immediately after the morning meal.”

Oliver watched as Matron O’Brien read from her notepad. He was startled to hear his own name called, since he had only been listening half-heartedly. He never expected that she would be talking about him. Now where had she said they were going? Did she mention how long they would be there? He knew he didn’t dare ask any questions and since he did hear her say to go to the Administration Building after breakfast tomorrow, he figured he would just do that. He’d have to figure the rest out later.

Arriving with four of his housemates at the big Administration Building the following morning, Oliver was surprised to see what looked like about thirty children clustered about the front lawn. There were boys of all ages; even a few babies in the arms of several matrons. Before long, a man who introduced himself as their “escort” began to read off their names.

"I wonder what an escort is," Oliver considered to himself.

That thought was quickly replaced by the call of, "Oliver Nordmark.... Edward Nordmark."

Oliver could not believe his ears. Edward was here too! Frantically Oliver began to look around among the crowd trying to locate Edward. Weaving in and around the other children, he finally spotted Edward at the side of a matron who held one of the babies. No longer looking like a baby himself, Edward had grown quite a bit in the year since Oliver had last seen him. But there was no mistaking those silky blond curls – it was Edward alright.

Quickly taking him by the hand, Oliver looked up very matter-of-factly at the matron and announced, "I'm Oliver Nordmark, Edward's big brother."

The matron cast a downward glance at Oliver. She quickly dropped Edward's hand saying, "Oh good. You keep a hold of him and see that he doesn't get lost."

Oliver spent the next few minutes reacquainting himself with Edward who seemed a bit surprised at this change of guardians. Ever so slowly the surprise was replaced with a faint recognition of a face from the past. After all, a year seems like a lifetime when you're just short of five years old!

Before long, the children were being led to two horse-drawn flatbed wagons. They climbed aboard to begin the first leg of the journey that surely would change their lives. Oliver sat with Edward between his legs. So many conflicting feelings and emotions were welling up inside him that he thought he might burst. He was scared. He was sad. He was thrilled to have Edward back at his side. He was apprehensive that perhaps the two of them would be separated again. He was excited to discover what might lay ahead for them. Quietly, to himself, Oliver made his decision. He would stick with being excited about the possible adventures that lay ahead. After all, nothing ventured, nothing gained. Isn't that what his father had always said? Ah, his father....Oliver hoped that his father would be proud of him for taking Edward under his wing. He hoped his mum, who Oliver imagined must be an angel by now, would watch out for her little boys and keep them out of harm's way.

After a short wagon ride, the orphans pulled into the crowded train station. There were other children there as well. Both boys and girls would be making this journey. Oliver thought of his sister Anna as his eyes darted about, searching. But Anna was nowhere to be found. I won't think of that now, thought Oliver. The boys from the wagons were led to the boxcars at the back of the train. They climbed aboard and settled into the soft hay that covered the floor, ready for whatever lay ahead.

CHAPTER SEVEN
KANSAS OR BUST!

As they awoke on the third day of their journey west, Oliver and Edward made a pact.

"We have to stay together no matter what," said Oliver.

"No matter what," Edward repeated.

"You're not a baby anymore Edward. So if they split up the babies from the boys, you're a big boy now," Oliver reasoned out loud. "You let me do the talking."

"Oliver talks," repeated Edward.

Later that day, after a lunch of mustard sandwiches and warm milk, things seemed like they were about to change.

The boy's escort stepped into their boxcar announcing, "We'll be pulling into Nemaha County Station in about fifteen minutes. Now you boys get yourselves together and lookin' your best for the townspeople. Get those shirt tails tucked in and pull your socks up. And for Heaven's sake, make sure you don't have dirt on your faces!" With that he turned and left, leaving the boys exchanging questioning glances.

Slowly the escort's words began to sink in and the boys began the task of "getting themselves together". There were no mirrors, so they took turns spit shining one another's faces until they were satisfied that each boy was looking his best.

When the whistle blew, announcing the train's arrival at the Nemaha County Station, the boys stood, anxiously peering out the boxcar door for a glimpse of their destination. Stopping at the platform, the boys were led off the train and onto waiting wagons.

"Stay close by me now Edward," warned Oliver.

Edward followed his big brother's command staying so close he bumped into Oliver's leg with every step. The two of them climbed aboard the wagon, heads tossing left and right trying to take in all the sights.

This was a small town with dirt roads and wooden buildings. Each building had a wood pole staked out across the front. Some of the poles had horses tied to them. There were people walking about and children running in the street playing games with sticks. The wagons took the orphans to the far end of town where there stood a big building. Wide steps led up to the big front doors. Across the top of the doors, Oliver could read the words TURNER HALL - BERN OPERA HOUSE. Just under that he read out loud to no one, "Bern, Kansas." A sign nailed to the side of the door read, VAUDEVILLE PERFORMANCE FIRST SATURDAY OF EVERY MONTH. In front of the building there were many horses and buggys, flatbed wagons, and carts.

"What do we do?" asked a worried Edward.

"Just stay close to me. Here, take my hand," replied Oliver, sticking his hand into Edward's. "Don't worry, Edward. And remember, you're not a baby. You're a boy."

Edward followed Oliver up the stairs of the Opera House, and through the big doors. Once inside, the boys filed along a table where a gentleman asked their names and their ages.

"Oliver Nordmark. I'm nearly eight," Oliver stated loudly. The gentleman wrote Oliver's name and age on a piece of paper attached to a string.

"Around your neck with this," the man instructed. "Next?"

"Edward Nordmark," began Edward, trying to sound just like Oliver. "I'm nearly five so I'm a boy, not a baby."

"Well, indeed you are," replied the man with a smile. "Welcome to Kansas, Edward." He handed Edward his name and age on a paper like Oliver's and Edward quickly placed it around his neck.

"I'm *not* a baby," Edward repeated to himself as he followed Oliver and the other children onto the stage of the Opera House. There were chairs on the stage and the boys quickly sat down, looking all around and wondering what would happen next. Within minutes they had their answer.

After all the children were seated, men and women came into the Opera House and began walking up and down in front of the orphans looking them over. Some asked questions of the children, others just looked. One man and his wife stopped in front of Oliver and Edward.

"Are you brothers?" the man asked with a strong foreign accent.

"Yes," replied Oliver. "And we are staying together because I am in charge of Edward." Oliver tried his hardest to sound firm and very grown up. "His matron put me in charge of him when we left New York City and that was three days ago."

"Well, then I suppose that we are very lucky today. We are looking for two brothers to live on our farm and help us with the farm chores. I think that you two boys would make a fine choice," the farmer said with a smile.

He turned to his wife and quickly spoke a foreign language to her. She looked at Oliver and Edward, nodded her head, and turned to the farmer, answering him in the same strange tongue.

"Then it is settled," the farmer spoke in English. "Come with us boys."

Edward and Oliver rose from their seats, grinning to one another at their success at having been able to stay together.

CHAPTER EIGHT
FARM BOYS IN KANSAS

"I am Henry Blaur," began the farmer as he spoke to Oliver and Edward who sat close together in the back of the flatbed wagon.

The horse-drawn wagon, loaded with supplies from the General Store, rattled down the rocky path away from the little town of Bern, Kansas. The boys held tight to the sides of the wagon, and to each other, to keep from sliding about.

"This is my wife, Berta," the farmer continued. "But you will call her Mrs. Blaur."

"Yes, Sir," replied Oliver.

"We are here in this country from our motherland Germany, you see," began farmer Blaur. Oliver sensed a long story about to pour forth from his new guardian. "We are farming the land and raising animals for food. We have horses, hogs, cattle, chickens, and goats," he continued in his strong German accent. "There are many chores and since we have no children of our own, we need strong boys to help. Do you know how to do this farm work, boys?"

Oliver was dumbstruck. Not only did he have no clue about farm work, he had never even been near a farm. Of course he knew about horses, but he had never seen hogs, chickens or goats. He could remember eating chicken, but he was pretty sure that wouldn't count. What kind of chores could possibly have to do with chickens?

"Ah....well....not too much," Oliver finally managed to say. "But I'm sure me and Edward will learn real quick! We're good learners, that's for sure!"

Eventually the Blaur's horse and wagon turned onto a long lane. Peering out the sides, Oliver and Edward could see in the distance a house on one side of the lane and a big barn on the other side. There were wooden pens around the barn and a smaller building, like a miniature barn, between the house and the big barn.

"What's that small barn for?" Oliver asked excitedly.

"Now that is the chicken coop," replied Mrs. Blaur. "One of your chores will be to gather the eggs that the chickens lay. Come with me," she said as the wagon pulled to a stop at the end of the lane. "I'll show you just what I mean."

All set for their newest adventure, Oliver and Edward climbed over the sides of the wagon and raced each other to the chicken coop. Just outside the door of the coop the boys found a wire pen that was full of baby chicks. Unable to contain his excitement, Oliver reached in and picked up a baby chick.

“Fly little birdie, fly!” he exclaimed as he tossed the chick into the air as high as he could.

Much to Oliver and Edward’s dismay, the chick did not fly. Instead, it came crashing to the ground at the boy’s feet and lay lifeless in the dirt.

“Oh! You little street urchin!” screamed Mrs. Blaur. “You stupid, stupid boy! A baby chick does not fly like a bird!” She stormed off into the farmhouse leaving the boys and Mr. Blaur standing alone with the fallen chick.

Oliver felt just terrible. He had no idea that baby chicks could not fly. All of a sudden he did not feel so good about this farm adventure anymore.

“They were so cute….” Oliver began in explanation to Mr. Blaur. “I was just gonna teach it to fly. You can bet I won’t do that anymore. I feel so bad about that baby chick.”

“You’ll learn,” replied Mr. Blaur as he bent and scooped up the dead chick. “You’ll learn.”

***

Early the next morning, Oliver and Edward were surprised to be woken from a deep sleep at 5:00AM.

“Come along boys,” shouted Mrs. Blaur. “Out of your beds now. There is much work to do.”

Rubbing their eyes with the back of their hands, the boys pushed back the blanket and stretched their little legs to meet the wooden floor. Finding their way down the stairs to the kitchen, Oliver and Edward saw two bowls of oatmeal on the table.

"Go and wash up now you two," Mrs. Blaur directed. "You will not be eating at my table with dirty hands."

"Yes Mrs. Blaur," the boys replied in unison.

After a quick washing at the water pump, the boys settled down to their first breakfast in their new home. Adding lots of sugar, Oliver and Edward took little time finishing what Mrs. Blaur had put in their bowls.

"Alright then boys, follow me now," called Mrs. Blaur over her shoulder as she exited the kitchen.

Oliver and Edward dutifully followed as Mrs. Blaur led them to the chicken coop.

"Your first task every morning will be to collect the eggs from the chickens," began Mrs. Blaur. "You reach under the hen like this," she demonstrated. "Then place the eggs carefully into your basket. Every week you will clean the chicken coop. You will remove the manure and wipe down the perches. Do you see these small bugs?" she questioned.

Two small heads nodded up and down.

"These are mites," Mrs. Blaur stated. "You must paint these with a brush dipped into the creosote bucket over there. It is the only way to kill them."

"Yuck," thought Oliver to himself.

"Yuck," said Edward out loud.

"Remember, every week this must be done," repeated Mrs. Blaur. "Now get to work!" She turned and left the chicken coop leaving Oliver and Edward alone.

"Well Edward, lets get to work then," smiled Oliver to his little brother. "We're farmers now, and this is farmer's work. I think it looks like fun."

Slowly the boys got the hang of gathering eggs from the hens and placing them into their baskets. They cleaned up the droppings with small metal shovels they found sticking out of a bucket in the corner of the coop. They cleaned off the perches as best they could with an old rag, and then carefully began the task of painting the creosote onto the perches. It left a bad smell and the boys were anxious to be finished and get out of there.

"Hey, Edward!" whispered Oliver as they reached the back of the chicken coop. "I got an idea!"

"What?" wondered Edward.

"Put an egg in each of your pockets, like this," began Oliver. "Leave your basket here and follow me!"

Edward followed Oliver's lead and tucked an egg deep into each of his pockets then hurried to catch up with his big brother.

Running around to the back of the big red barn where no one would see them, Oliver and Edward took turns tossing the eggs as high as they could against the side of the barn. Laughing and giggling, they watched as the yellow yolks ran down the side of the big red barn.

"Maybe there's something to this farm life after all!" laughed Oliver as he and Edward smiled at each other.

"Yep!" replied Edward, "This is fun being farmers!"

****

The next morning was a hot, sunny Wednesday and Oliver and Edward quickly rushed through breakfast and out to gather the eggs from the chicken coop. They had intended to have some more fun behind the barn, but on their way they heard a strange noise.

"Woo, Woo, Woo, Woo," came the noise from the back of the barn.

"What was that?" asked Edward tentatively.

"Let's go see!" answered Oliver, always looking for adventure.

Walking through the barn, they continued to hear the strange sound. When they reached the back of the barn they saw a pen full of short fat animals.

"What are them animals, Oliver?" Edward wondered.

"I think it must be hogs, but I don't know for sure, I never seen a real hog before," Oliver replied. "Hey, I got an idea, Edward. Come on!"

The boys ran back into the barn and picked up some long slats that were used to cover cracks on the barn walls. Quietly they snuck into the pen of hogs and started poking and chasing them around and around.

"Woo, Woo, Woo," squealed the pigs, making quite a racket.

Mr. and Mrs. Blaur came running out of the farmhouse. At just that very minute, the man from New York who had escorted the boys on the train pulled up in a horse-drawn buggy. He was stopping by to check on the boys before he left town. Seeing the panic on the Blaur's faces, he jumped from his buggy and joined them on their race to the barn.

"Oliver! Edward!" shouted Mr. Blaur. "Stop that right now, do you hear me?"

The boys ended their chase and tossed down their boards. Unfortunately, it was too late for the largest of the hogs. The heat of the sun and the chasing around was just too much. The hog plopped himself down in a mud puddle and died.

"Ahh!" gasped Oliver and Edward, alarmed at this latest development.

They looked at the Blaurs and the man from New York with their innocent faces, for surely they had no idea that running would cause a hog to die.

Oliver leaned slightly in Edward's direction and whispered, "We might just get a whippin' for this Edward."

CHAPTER NINE
LIFE TURNS AGAIN

Much to their surprise, there was no whipping issued for pig chasing that day. They were, however, admonished for their behavior and told not to do anything like that again. They were immediately sent into a nearby field to pull weeds – pigweed it was called – that would be used as feed for the hogs.

Oliver and Edward tried hard to enjoy themselves on the Kansas farm. There were many chores and the boys often went to bed exhausted and without enough to eat. But somehow they always found a way to have a little fun.

About six months after their arrival and placement at the Blaur's farm, Oliver began to notice things that set his mind thinking. He felt no real affection from his guardians. In fact, the Blaurs were often angry and annoyed with their new charges – especially Mrs. Blaur.

"You boys come down here for your lunch right now or there will be no food for you," Mrs. Blaur shouted up the stairs one cold winter afternoon. It was Saturday and the boys had finished their morning chores early. They had retreated to their room to get out of the cold and had just started a game of marbles on the wooden floor when the shouting started.

Knowing that she meant business, and knowing that there would be more chores after lunch, Oliver and Edward quickly pushed their game under the bed and ran down to the kitchen.

"Now eat that," said Mrs. Blaur as she pushed a tin bowl of soup in front of the boys. "Then get yourselves out to the barn and clean those stalls. There's plenty more to do when that's done so don't waste time."

Looking down at the grease floating on top of the soup, Oliver remembered what he had learned in the orphanage and checked his tongue. He knew better than to complain about food....or even to ask questions for that matter. Edward, on the other hand, had not learned this lesson.

"This is bad! I don't like it," he whined.

Taking Edward by the hair, Mrs. Blaur pushed his face towards the bowl and snarled, "You'll eat it and be thankful that you have anything to eat at all!"

Silently Edward began eating the soup, glancing up at Oliver with a sick look on his face. Oliver, too, continued to eat the greasy soup. About half way through his bowl, Oliver felt his stomach churning. Rushing from his seat, he headed straight to the coal bucket in the corner and vomited. His chest heaved and his throat felt as though it would choke as the retching continued. Finally the agony began to subside and Oliver stumbled back to his seat.

"You don't like the soup? Fine. You can eat with the dogs!" shouted a very angry Mrs. Blaur.

Oliver couldn't believe his ears. He knew exactly what the six dogs that lived on the Blaur's farm ate. At butchering time, the rinds were saved. The lard was boiled out of the rinds and food scraps and corn meal were stirred in to make dog food. Slowly Edward and Oliver rose from the table and went to the pantry. Old brown paper scraps were kept there to feed the dogs on. Oliver went into the pantry first and retrieved a paper. As he left the pantry with his head down, Edward went to get his paper. Not being able to face eating dog food, little Edward glanced up and saw the pantry window. Without even thinking, he pushed open the sill and climbed out into the cold. As soon as his feet hit the ground, he took off like a shot in the direction of town. Mrs. Blaur waited only a few seconds then followed Edward into the pantry.

Seeing the open window, she stuck her head out and bellowed, "You come back here or I'll get the hounds after you!"

Poor little Edward! He was afraid of the dogs when they were standing still….he was petrified of being chased by them. Crying and sobbing, tears streaming down his face, Edward turned and ran back to the house.

Mrs. Blaur changed her mind about the boys eating with the dogs that day. Instead she handed each a crust of bread and shooed them out to the barn to begin their afternoon chores.

****

The only respite that Edward and Oliver got from Mr. and Mrs. Blaur was the time they spent in school. Shortly after their arrival in Kansas, Mr. Blaur took the boys to the schoolhouse to begin their studies. Riding in the back of the farmer's wagon, Oliver and Edward enjoyed looking around at their new surroundings, breathing in the fresh clean air. When the first school day came to an end, Oliver and Edward ran from the building expecting to see Mr. Blaur's wagon to take them home. Not seeing their ride, they sat down under a nearby tree to wait. No wagon arrived and finally their new teacher came out of the schoolhouse.

"What are you two boys up to, just sittin' there?" she asked.

"We're waiting for our wagon ride home," replied Oliver.

"I'd say your waiting is over. No wagon is coming for you so you'd better start walking," their teacher replied as she turned and disappeared around the corner of the building.

Oliver and Edward looked at one another, shrugged their shoulders and got up to start the trek home. Oliver soon began to regret not paying closer attention to the route they had taken to school that morning. They climbed what seemed to them like a mountain of a hill, and then walked along the top of that hill for quite a distance.

"How much further," complained Edward. "I'm tired and my feet hurt!"

"Not too much further," Oliver lied.

Coming down the other side of the hill, they walked through a valley then came to a crick.

"We didn't cross no crick in the wagon, Oliver," warned Edward. "You got us lost!"

"I know we didn't cross a crick Edward. We're taking a short cut," lied Oliver again. "Now stop complaining and keep up with me!"

Finding a place that seemed shallow enough to cross, Edward and Oliver made their way across stepping stones, trying hard to keep their shoes dry. The other side of the crick was quite rugged and the boys stumbled repeatedly, but kept moving on.

Finally they came to a wagon path that, to Oliver, looked somewhat familiar. Taking a chance, he decided that they would follow that path. After what seemed like hours, they arrived dusty and exhausted at a turn in the path that Oliver was now *sure* he recognized.

"This way, Edward!" he shouted as he began to run with renewed energy.

"Wait for me!" Edward moaned as he too began to run to keep up with his big brother. "Don't leave me!"

At last the boys arrived back at the Blaur's farm. Running up to Mr. Blaur outside the chicken coop, Oliver expected the man to be very apologetic for having forgotten to retrieve them.

"Now that took you longer than it should have," began farmer Blaur. "Next time get yourselves straight back here after school. There's chores to do you know. It shouldn't be taking you that long to walk just one mile."

"One mile!" thought Oliver to himself. "*Just* one mile!"

The boys both paid closer attention the following day on their wagon ride to school. This time they found their way back with no trouble when classes had ended. By the end of the week they were walking both ways and enjoying their time alone together.

****

As much as they enjoyed their time going to and from school, being *at* school quickly became hard for Oliver and Edward. Since they spoke differently than the other children because of their New York accents, they were often picked on and made fun of.

"Hey city boys!" taunted a particularly mean boy one morning in the school yard. "No one ever taught you to speak English straight? I guess no one to teach ya, bein' as you got no ma or pa."

Laughter and snickering erupted from the small crowd of boys encircling the brothers.

"Oh yeah! Who says I can't speak English?" Oliver fumed back at the bully. "This should speak clearly enough!" he shouted as he lunged his tin lunch bucket towards the offender.

The bully took the hit square on his left knee and as he started to stagger, Oliver dropped the bucket and dove onto the boy with fists flying. Just as Oliver was clearly getting the better of his opponent, their teacher saw what was happening and came running.

"Stop that fighting now!" she commanded. "Do you hear me, I said NOW!" She tugged at the boys who broke apart from one another, eyes glaring. "There will be no more of that from the two of you. If there is, it will mean expulsion. Now inside with all of you."

The boys headed for the schoolhouse with Oliver and Edward lagging behind.

"You really showed him, Oliver!" Edward praised his big brother. "You were winning that fight, that's for sure!"

Oliver just shrugged his shoulders and followed Edward inside. Although they continued to be picked on now and again, everyone knew not to push it too hard. Oliver had proven that he wasn't afraid of any of them and he would fight for himself and for his brother if that was what he had to do.

****

During the bitter cold January of 1907, something happened that convinced Oliver that things were going to change for him and Edward. After their morning trek to school, the boys watched with their classmates from the schoolhouse windows as the skies took on a menacing shade of grey. Before long the dark clouds had opened up and swirling snow began to fall. The students were all excited as they dreamed of the fun they would have in the snow once school was out. As the hours wore on, the winds picked up and the snow fell harder and harder.

Looking warily out at the storm, the boy's teacher made a quick decision. "Class dismissed students," she announced. "We'll all need time to get home before this storm becomes dangerous."

Cheering shouts erupted from the class as all the students jumped from their seats and raced outside.

Once outside, the sheering winds ripped right through Oliver and Edward as they anxiously looked around, hoping to see farmer Blaur. Seeing no one, and seeing no wagon in sight, they did the only thing they knew to do.

"Pull your stocking cap down as far as it will go, Edward." Oliver instructed. "We're going to have to start walking. I'm sure farmer Blaur will be along shortly. He's probably trying to get through the snow right now."

"But he doesn't know that school ended early," protested Edward. "He's not coming for us. He never comes for us."

Oliver considered this possibility but quickly dismissed it. "This is a blizzard, Edward. Even farmer Blaur knows we could never walk a mile home in a blizzard. He'll come. Let's get started. We'll stay warmer if we're moving. We'll freeze if we just stand here waiting."

Even though he wasn't really following Oliver's reasoning, Edward fell in behind his brother and started the trip home. It wasn't long before the two boys could see nothing behind them and nothing ahead of them. The schoolhouse disappeared in the flying snow. The wind was blowing so strongly that Oliver could hardly see ten feet in front of himself. The only way he knew where he was going was to watch the ridge of the hill and then to follow the river bank of the crick.

Edward held tight to the back of Oliver's coat so as not to get separated in the storm. Both boys felt frozen to the core.

"We're going to die in the snow Oliver!" Edward cried.

"No Edward, we will not die. But we *are* cold. When farmer Blaur finds us he'll take us to the farmhouse and warm us with hot coffee," replied Oliver. Secretly, Oliver did not believe a word of his comfort to Edward. Although he found it nearly impossible to believe, he instinctively knew that no one was coming for them. No one ever came for them….not even in a blizzard.

Finally making it to the Blaur's farmhouse, Oliver and Edward fell exhausted and freezing through the front door.

"Come on now boys!" Mrs. Blaur called out. "Get those wet things off before they drip all over everything."

Oliver could not believe his ears. No apology…no concern….no comfort.

"The only one looking out for us," Oliver thought to himself, "Is us. Now there's a lesson I've finally learned. We are on our own, whether we live on this farm or in New York City. We are on our own." It was a lesson that Oliver would remember until the day he died.

CHAPTER TEN

DON'T FORGET ME EDWARD

Slowly the deep cold of winter began to fade. The days began to get longer and little signs of spring started popping up all around the farm. As Oliver and Edward watched farmer Blaur begin to till the soil for the spring planting, Oliver had the idea that he wanted to plant a garden of his own.

"I have no seed to spare for such folly," farmer Blaur replied when Oliver went to him for some seeds to plant.

"If I find some seeds of my own, can I plant them," Oliver asked hopefully.

"I don't know where you would find any but if you do, yes you can plant them behind the chicken coop," the farmer replied.

"Now where can I find seeds," thought Oliver to himself. He thought about planting kernels of corn, but he decided that probably wouldn't work. Maybe he could plant cucumber seeds. But what would be the sense in that? Even if they did grow, Oliver didn't like cucumbers. No, he wanted to plant something that would grow just for him and Edward to eat.

Cantaloupe! That's what he would plant. Both Oliver and Edward loved the sweet taste of fresh cantaloupe.

The next morning when cantaloupe was on the breakfast table, Oliver put his plan into motion.

"I'd be happy to help cut that cantaloupe, Mrs. Blaur," offered Oliver. "I'm getting bigger now and I can handle a cutting knife."

Mrs. Blaur looked suspiciously towards Oliver. Not imagining what he could be up to, and not caring to do more than necessary for the boys, she nodded her head yes.

Oliver jumped from his seat and carefully took the sharp knife into his hand. Very slowly he pushed the knife through the center of the fruit and gently separated the two halves. When he was sure Mrs. Blaur was not looking, Oliver scooped a handful of the seeds from the cantaloupe and quickly slid them into his pocket. Of course he wasn't sure if he would get in trouble should she see him, but you could never tell with Mrs. Blaur. Best to be on the safe side and not let her see, Oliver reasoned.

Shortly before lunch, when the morning chores had been completed, Oliver had some free time. He ran behind the chicken coop with his pocketful of seeds and began to dig with one of the shovels from the coop.

"Whatcha up to?" Edward asked.

"Oh, Edward, you scared me!" a startled Oliver replied. "I'm making a garden of cantaloupe just for me and you."

"When can we eat them?" Edward wanted to know.

"It will take awhile for them to grow," Oliver replied. "I'm not really sure, but probably sometime in the summer."

"Can I help?" asked Edward.

Oliver smiled, handing Edward his shovel as he ran into the chicken coop for a second one. The boys worked busily on their garden. They planted the seeds in rows, carefully covering them and watering them. Then Oliver got some old chicken wire from the coop and pushed it into the ground all around their little garden.

"That should do it," Oliver proudly stated as he and Edward stood back to look at their work.

"Yep! That should do it." Edward repeated.

Smiling at one another, they ran off towards the farmhouse for lunch.

****

Every day for the next few weeks Oliver would sneak behind the chicken coop to check on his garden. He was elated the morning he saw tiny green sprouts reaching up through the soil. Spring gradually turned to summer and the sprouts grew into small plants. Oliver was anxious and excited to see if the plants would actually bear fruit.

On the morning of July 2nd, just two days before the big 4th of July celebration in Bern, Oliver and Edward woke to some unexpected news.

"Out of the bed you two," Mrs. Blaur nudged the boys. "That man from the Children's Aid Society is on his way for you right now, so get ready."

"Ready for what?" a groggy Oliver asked.

"He's taking you to a new family. We cannot care for you any longer," Mrs. Blaur said flatly.

Without a word, Oliver and Edward rose from their bed and quickly dressed for the day. They reached under the bed for their small carrying case and haphazardly stuffed their few belongings into it. The boys stumbled down the stairs to the kitchen and sat quietly as they ate their breakfast. Once finished, they walked outside and sat stiffly on the front step of the farmhouse.

"Where will we go?" Edward wanted to know.

"I don't know, Edward," replied Oliver looking slowly around the Blaur farm. "But wherever it is, I bet it will be better than living here."

"Can we take our garden with us?" Edward wondered as he looked sadly towards the chicken coop.

"No, Edward, you can't carry a garden with you."

"We'll stick together, right Oliver?" questioned Edward, his lip quivering.

"We're brothers Edward, we'll stick together," Oliver reassured him.

Before long the horse-drawn wagon from The Children's Aid Society pulled into the farmhouse lane and the boys stood up, holding their belongings.

"Come along boys, climb in," the man said trying to sound cheery.

Silently Oliver and Edward climbed into the wagon. As it pulled away from the Blaur farm, Oliver looked over his shoulder expecting to wave goodbye. But Mrs. Blaur never came out of the house. Looking towards the barn, Oliver could see farmer Blaur feeding the hogs. He never looked up as the wagon went by. If he had, he would have seen two quiet and frightened boys huddled together, trying to become one.

****

The wagon carried Oliver and Edward back to the town of Bern. It stopped at the train station where the man instructed the boys to gather their things and come with him.

"The train will be coming for you soon," began the man. "You will ride with more children further west. The next stop will be Mankato, about a hundred and fifty miles I'd say."

Not knowing what to say, the boys silently awaited the train's arrival. They climbed aboard and settled in for the hundred and fifty mile trek.

Arriving in Mankato, Oliver and Edward followed very much the same routine as they had upon their arrival in Bern, Kansas a year before. They lined up on the Opera House stage with their name tags around their necks and waited to be picked by one of the farmers now inspecting the children.

"I'm Frank McCammon," a gruff voice announced in Oliver's direction. "I think you'll do just fine." He placed a hand on Oliver's shoulder but Oliver jerked back in his seat.

"Me and Edward are brothers and we're staying together," Oliver boldly announced, figuring he had nothing to lose.

"Well, I'm afraid I got no use for a young one like him," Mr. McCammon replied, glancing in Edward's direction. "He couldn't do the kind of work I got in mind."

As Edward's face flushed in fear, and tears began to fill the corners of his eyes, an old man poked his head into their conversation.

"Well, Frank, I reckon I could take the little fellow home with me. You're not more than a day's ride from my place. I'm sure we could let the boys visit with each other now and again," spoke the older farmer. “Name’s Gish. William Gish. But you can just call me Gish,” he introduced himself to Edward, extending his right hand.

Taking the wrinkled hand in his, Edward heard himself softly say, “I’m Edward Nordmark and I’m nearly six.”

“Well then, Edward, have we got a deal?” William Gish smiled.

Looking towards his brother, Edward searched for the answer in Oliver’s eyes. As his heart sank, Oliver nodded in Edward’s direction. He knew that these people could separate them no matter what Oliver and Edward wanted and at least these two farmers lived fairly close to one another. If Edward didn’t find a home here in Mankato and had to get back on the train, there would be no telling how far apart the two of them would be.

“It’s a deal,” Oliver spoke up for his brother. “But only if we get to see each other at least four times a year.”

Both farmers nodded their agreement and the four of them headed out of the Opera House. As their wagons headed off in different directions, Oliver tried to stay brave for little Edward.

“Don’t forget me, Edward!” he called out to farmer Gish’s wagon with a forced smile. “Never forget me!”

CHAPTER ELEVEN

OLIVER ON HIS OWN

Frank McCammon's wagon traveled ten miles west of Mankato that day to his farm in Esbon, Kansas. William Gish's wagon headed south for twelve miles to Ionia, Kansas. Despite their agreement in the Opera House, Oliver and Edward visited with one another only one time over the next seven years. Oliver spent those years as a farm hand. He worked hard, learning all the skills needed to be a successful farmer. By age fifteen, he was responsible for most all the daily work. Any spare time was spent on his studies. All that changed on July 4, 1913.

Oliver rose, as usual, before the sun. He strapped on his overalls and headed to the barn for the morning milking. He met up with Mr. McCammon outside the barn when the milking was complete.

"Come and help me hitch up my wagon, Oliver," McCammon called out. "Me and the wife are headed up to my brother's place for a visit. When you're done with all the chores you're welcome to go into town and meet up with your friends. There's gonna be a big 4th of

July celebration, ya know. Maybe even some fireworks."

"Sure thing," replied Oliver, excited at the idea of having some fun. "I'll get everything done."

Oliver watched as the wagon carrying McCammon and his wife pulled off. He quickly turned to get started with the day's work. He fed and watered McCammon's dog, fed the hogs and cows, mucked out the horse stalls and cleaned the perches of the chicken coop. It was nearly noon before he got everything finished.

Oliver had a pony in the barn and he headed off to saddle her up. It wasn't *really* Oliver's pony, but for the time being, it may as well be. McCammon's brother actually owned the pony. It was kind of stunted and would never get very big so he had asked Oliver if he would break the horse in for one of his kids to ride. Oliver agreed to the task. He kept the pony in the barn and was real nice to it. He gave it the best hay he could find and plenty of grain. He kept the pony clean and brushed it often. To break the pony for riding, he first put just the saddle blanket on her. After awhile, he put the saddle on top of the blanket and let her walk around with it on her back for many days. Eventually, he took to riding the pony. She settled down rather quickly to the feel of Oliver on her back and soon he was riding the pony all over. McCammon's brother hadn't yet come to take the pony back, and Oliver wasn't about to offer to give her up. And so it was that on July 4th, fifteen-year-old Oliver saddled up his pony and headed into town.

****

It was a seven mile ride into town and Oliver rode like the wind to get there as fast as he could. He quickly met up with some of the boys he knew from school who also had come to town for the festivities.

"Hey, Oliver!" called out a lanky boy by the name of Hank. "Hitch up that sorry excuse for a horse of yours and get down here. We're fixin' to have a little fun!"

"Be right there. And watch what you say about my pony. She can outrun anything you might be riding!" Oliver joked as he headed for the livery stable.

After dismounting and checking in with the stable hand, Oliver ran off to join his friends.

"Come on," Hank motioned to the boys. "Let's get us each a cigar to celebrate!"

Into the General Store they went. Oliver looked around, knowing he only had about half a dollar in his pocket. He was feeling a bit hungry but decided to save his money and just get a cigar with his friends. After each boy made his purchase, they headed out behind the shops and down over a small embankment to walk along the creek.

"What took you so long gettin' into town, Oliver?" asked his friend Billy.

"Oh, you know, McCammon had to go visit his brother which left all the work for me. I got things done just as quick as I could, but I gotta tell you, he's gettin' lazier all the time. If it weren't for me, I bet that whole farm would come falling down around him."

"So get out," Hank offered. "If I was you I'd run off and look to stake out my own claim. He ain't got no hold on you. He ain't your pa or nothin'."

"That he ain't," mused Oliver as he took a .22 revolver from inside his jacket.

"Now how in the blazes did you get that," gasped Billy. "You steal that or somethin'?"

"No, I didn't steal it," Oliver indignantly replied. "I ordered it from Montgomery Ward. Right out of their catalog."

"Oh yeah!" replied Billy, certain that he was lying. "Like McCammon would ever let you keep a gun that was delivered to the farm."

Oliver glanced in Hank's direction and noticed him grinning and shuffling his feet in the dirt. "You're right Billy," Oliver smiled, quite full of himself. "That's why I was smart enough to have them send it to Hank's place. This ain't just a pretty face ya know. Clever, that's me!"

"Okay, then, if you're so clever, let me see you hit that piece of fence post on the other side of the creek," challenged Billy.

Oliver grinned. Raising the revolver straight out in front of him, he slowly took aim and fired off a shot that hit the post square on.

"Nothin' to it," Oliver boasted. "I can hit a matchstick - that is if you care to hold it!"

"Whooo-Waaa, Whooo-Waaa," sounded the incoming freight train, grabbing the boy's attention.

"Come on!" shouted Hank, running in the direction of the low whistle. "Let's jump it!"

All the boys headed off in the train's direction, trying to catch up with Hank. Reaching the tracks, they ran along with the slowing train. As they shoved their cigars in their mouths, one by one the boys jumped onto the side of the train.

"We're ridin' the rails!" someone called out in glee.

All at once, as the train slowed to a stop, an idea came into Oliver's head. It hit him hard.

"Geez!" he thought to himself. "Here's my chance to get out of here!"

He made up his mind just that quick. Without a word to his friends, who were laughing and joking about their ride, Oliver ran straight to the General Store.

"A pound of gingersnaps, please," Oliver asked the clerk. He paid for them, and looked down to see that he had but twenty-three cents left. He quickly shoved the coins into his pocket and ran from the store with the gingersnaps.

Glancing in the direction of the livery stable, Oliver thought about the pony. He knew he should take her back to McCammon's barn, but if he did that he was sure to miss his opportunity.

"Sorry 'bout that McCammon," he murmured to himself.

Running towards the train, Oliver crossed the tracks and lay down in the tall weeds. He figured about ten to fifteen minutes went by before he heard the calling of the freight train's whistle announcing its departure from the station.

Only a moment of hesitation ran though his head as he thought about what he was about to do. He quickly dismissed any thoughts that would have changed his mind. As the freight train slowly began chugging along the tracks away from the platform, Oliver jumped from his hiding place and started chasing the engine.

"I got me a life to lead," he could hear himself saying. "Nothin' ventured, nothin' gained!" And with that, Oliver reached up to the steel handles behind the train's locomotive and pulled himself aboard.

The freight train pulled out of Esbon, Kansas late on the afternoon of July 4, 1913 with young Oliver Nordmark hitched aboard. Although he never saw the town's fireworks that evening, he was certain that he felt as much excitement as any of his friends. Like a bird taking flight, Oliver was anxious to find his own way in the world…..and maybe even a lost brother.

About The Author

A resident of Hockessin Delaware, Donna Nordmark Aviles is the 19th grandchild of Oliver and Estella Nordmark. She is the author of three books for 9-12 year olds and enjoys visiting schools and community organizations to educate audiences on the Orphan Train Movement of 1854-1929.

Her first two books, *Fly Little Bird, Fly!* and *Beyond The Orphan Train* are based on Oliver's oral history and were named the WINNER of the 2009 Best Books Award sponsored by USA Book News – Audiobook Format.

Her third book, *Peanut Butter For Cupcakes: A True Story From The Great Depression,* was named the WINNER of the 2009 National Literary Foundation's Christopher Robin Award for Children's Literature. Additionally, it was named a Finalist in the 2009 Next Generation Indie Book Awards. Based on oral histories of Oliver's three surviving sons, it is the story of their childhood years with Oliver during the 1930's.

To learn more about Donna Nordmark Aviles, The Orphan Train Movement, and how to schedule an author visit, go to: **www.orphantrainbook.com**.

*"**Fly Little Bird, Fly!** and **Beyond The Orphan Train** are two books that cover an important but little known part of U.S. history. Understanding the settlement of the Plains from a personal perspective is a powerful method of teaching."*

- Peter N. Jones, PhD – Cultural Anthropologist

Breinigsville, PA USA
18 February 2011
255893BV00001B/2/P